VACATION'S OVER! RETURN OF THE DINOSAURS

JOE KULKA

CAROLRHODA BOOKS MINNEAPOLIS

Carolrhoda Books
A division of Lerner Publishing Group, Inc.
241 First Avenue North
Minneapolis, MN 55401 U.S.A.

Website address: www.lernerbooks.com

Library of Congress Cataloging-in-Publication Data

Kulka, Joe.
    Vacation's over! : return of the dinosaurs / by Joe Kulka ;
illustrations by Joe Kulka.
       p.   cm.
    Summary: Relates what happened to the dinosaurs who
escaped extinction.
    ISBN: 978-0-7613-5212-9 (lib. bdg. : alk. paper)
    [1. Stories in rhyme. 2. Dinosaurs—Fiction. 3. Humorous
stories.] I. Title. II. Title: Vacation is over.
PZ8.3.K9449Va 2010
[E]—dc22   2009034277

Manufactured in the United States of America
1 - DP - 7/15/10

For James, Michael, and Kaitlyn

TYRANNOSAURUS REX

DINOSAURS
are gone forever, fossilized and extinct.

They never
will return
again—

so is
that what
you think?

Well, long ago
spaceships came...

and took them on a cruise.

Now they are on their way back home.
So spread the happy news!

FREE
SPACE
CRUISE

They spent the last few million years rocketing past the stars, visiting some distant planets like Jupiter and Mars.

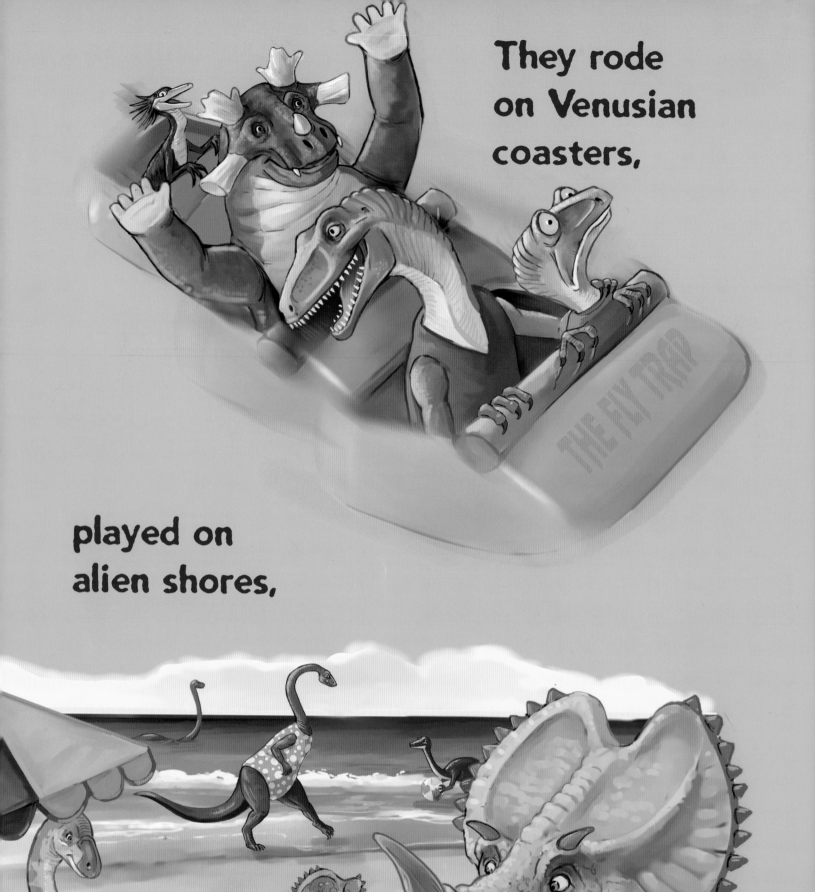

They rode
on Venusian
coasters,

played on
alien shores,

indulged in the lavish buffets,
and took all the scenic tours.

Returned
from their
long vacation,
greeted with
cheers and grins,

dinos are now
everywhere.
Time to
settle back in.

On the wrong side of
the Great Wall,

a dino
starts to
roar.

Famished after their long ride home,
the menu makes them fret.
The escargot looks quite tasty;
their waiter, better yet.

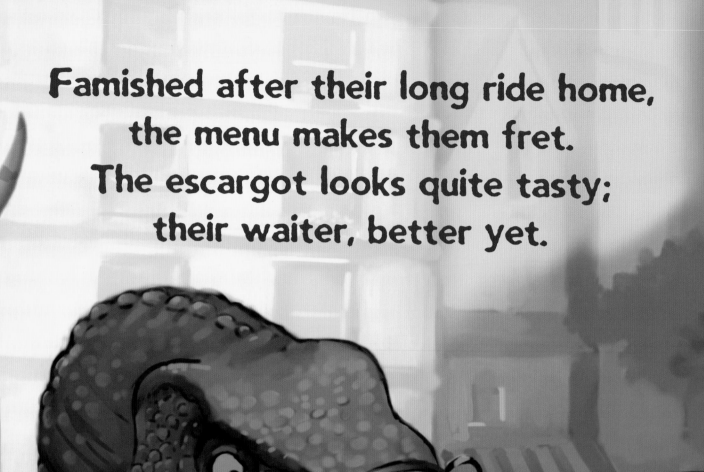

T. rex finds his
cave is the same,
but inside, he has
an awful shock:
his little pet
Fluffy Foo Foo
is now a
fluffy rock.

Need to get some new school supplies. Let's head out to the mall.

Got our pencils
and our paper.
Gosh! They're
awfully small.

Rolls and rolls of film developed.
Half the photos blank!
"I told you so a thousand times!
Take off the lens cap, Frank!"

Staring out at the
rain forest,
a dinosaur just sighs.
His lawn grew way
out of control
with weeds that
reach the sky.

G. MIMUS

Hanging up loads of soaking wash
on a hot Kenyan plain,
a dino mumbles to herself,
"Won't pack so much again."

Dreaming of his next vacation, Rex smiles as he snores. Good to have you back home again, so sleep well, dinosaur.